KU-479-156

DIARY
OF A
CHRISTMAS
ELF

More magical adventures
from Ben Miller:

The Night I Met Father Christmas

The Boy Who Made the World Disappear

The Day I Fell into A Fairytale

How I Became a Dog Called Midnight

BEN MILLER

DIARY
OF A
CHRISTMAS
ELF

Illustrated by
Daniela Jaglenka Terrazzini

SIMON & SCHUSTER

First published in Great Britain in 2021 by Simon & Schuster UK Ltd
Text copyright © Passion Projects Limited 2021

Illustrations copyright © Daniela Jaglenka Terrazzini
This book is copyright under the Berne Convention.
No reproduction without permission.

3 5 7 9 10 8 6 4 2

Simon & Schuster UK Ltd
1st Floor, 222 Gray's Inn Road
London
WC1X 8HB

www.simonandschuster.co.uk

Simon & Schuster Australia, Sydney
Simon & Schuster India, New Delhi
A CIP catalogue record for this book is available from the British Library.

HB ISBN 978-1-3985-0183-6
Australian HB ISBN 978-1-3985-0207-9
eBook ISBN 978-1-3985-0184-3
Audio ISBN 978-1-3985-0186-7

Printed and bound by CPI Group (UK) Ltd, Croydon, CR0 4YY

MIX
Paper from
responsible sources
FSC® C020471
FSC
www.fsc.org

For Steph

Tuesday 21 October

L ast night I dreamed I was a Christmas Elf.

It was Christmas Day, and we were all at Father Christmas's lodge in the Arctic Hills, celebrating another successful year.

At one end of the room was a roaring fire, framed by garlands of holly, ivy and mistletoe; at the other sat Father Christmas, flanked by his Right-

Hand and Left-Hand Elves.

And in between sat the rest of us: row after row of red-faced Toymaking Elves, feasting, laughing and joking.

I was just tucking into my second turkey leg, when Father Christmas stood and tapped his glass with a spoon, to get our attention. We all fell silent.

'Dearest elves,' he said, sliding gracefully off his chair and on to his feet. Unfortunately he is quite short, so all we could see behind the table was his red velvet hat.

'Ah,' said Father Christmas thoughtfully.

Steinar, his Right-Hand Elf, and Ola, his Left-Hand Elf, helped him to stand on the seat of his chair. Father Christmas mopped his face with his handkerchief,

Father Christmas stood and tapped his glass

collected himself, and resumed his speech.

'You have worked tirelessly all year, and I am quite overwhelmed with gratitude. On behalf of all the children of the world, thank you, thank you, thank you!'

We all clinked glasses and drank huge mouthfuls of the most delicious mead.

'Now, I know what you're all wondering,' Father Christmas continued. 'Who can it be? Who is my Christmas Elf of the Year?'

The room filled with excited chatter.

'Well . . .'

An expectant hush descended.

'Without further delay . . .'

Everyone looked around the room.

'My Christmas Elf of the Year is . . .'

An elf on the far table let out a yelp of excitement.

'The one and only . . .'

Steinar, the Right-Hand Elf, cleared his throat, impatiently.

'. . . Tog!'

That was ME!! *I* was Christmas Elf of the Year!

The room burst into wild applause.

'Up you get . . .' said my mother.

But I couldn't seem to get up from the table! It was as if my bottom was glued to my seat.

'. . . Tog, get up! You're late!'

I opened my eyes. I wasn't in Father Christmas's house at all. I was in my bunk, in the tiny room I shared with my four younger brothers and sisters:

5

Twig, Leaf, Plum and Pin. My mother was shaking me by the shoulder.

'Your father and I are off to work! You need to get the little ones to school!'

Which was when I remembered who I really am: an unemployed one-hundred-and-sixty-year-old loser elf who is still living with his parents.

Oh, and just in case it's a human reading this (it's always possible): elves live ten times as long as humans. So one hundred and sixty to us is like sixteen to you.

Wednesday 22 October

Disaster. Plum has lost Oscar.

We only noticed when we got to the school gate.

Oscar is Plum's toy lemur. Father Christmas gave him to her when she was a baby, and he goes everywhere with her.

'She must have dropped him,' said Twig.

'In the snow,' said Leaf.

'Because we were rushing,' said Twig.

'Because you overslept,' added Pin, helpfully.

It was true, and I felt terrible.

'Don't worry, Plum,' I said. 'Socks will find him!' Socks is our pet husky, and her sense of smell is amazing.

'Pinky promise?' Plum sniffed.

'Pinky promise,' I said, and we solemnly shook fingers. No elf has ever broken a pinky promise.

Not until now, anyway.

Because even though I've searched *everywhere*, Oscar is nowhere to be found.

I even tried giving Socks one of Oscar's knitted jumpers to sniff, to tune her in to his scent, but I'm not sure she understood what I was asking for.

I'm such a failure.

All I have to do is walk my brothers and sisters to school, clean the house, buy the food for supper, cook it, walk them home, help them with their homework and get them ready for bed. And I can't even do that right.

And as for my dream of becoming a Christmas Elf . . .

Well, I suppose I should just forget it.

Thursday 23 October

S till no sign of Oscar.

I've searched everywhere, but he's vanished.

It's a long time until Christmas, and Plum has already had her birthday, so to stop her having to wait ages for a replacement, I've decided to take matters into my own hands.

After drop-off at school, I called in at the library.

They only have one book about lemurs, but luckily no one has ever borrowed it, so it was available.

My head is now full of lemur facts. It turns out that Oscar was a ring-tailed lemur. Did you know lemurs are only found on the Island of Madagascar, off the east coast of Africa? Their faces are white, with black patches around their eyes and noses, and they have grey bodies and white tummies. Oh, and tails circled with black-and-white rings. Which I guess is how they get their name.

Their favourite food is the leaf of the tamarind tree. And they love to sunbathe by sitting upright on their hind legs with their arms outstretched, which looks a bit like they are doing yoga.

I could go on . . .

Friday 24 October

I am so embarrassed.

Went to the craft shop with a list of all the things I need to make a lemur:

1. black, white and grey fur;
2. a fluffy black-and-white tail;
3. a black sew-on nose;
4. orange sew-on eyes.

While I was in there, I bumped into someone. Literally. Lots of electronics spilled out of her shopping bag, and I bent down to help her pick them all up.

'Sorry,' she said. 'I didn't see you there.' She had pale green eyes, freckles on her nose, and bright red hair.

'What are you making?' I asked her.

'A fixed-wing drone,' she replied. I think I must have looked confused because she added, 'It's like a multi-rotor drone, but with a much longer flying time. Plus, it can take a heavier payload.'

I had no idea what she was talking about, so I just nodded.

'How about you?' she asked. 'What are you making?'

'Sorry' she said. 'I didn't see you there'

'A lemur,' I replied. Now it was her turn to look puzzled. 'It's a kind of primate,' I said helpfully, 'that lives on the island of Madagascar.'

She still looked confused, so I kept talking. That may have been a mistake. 'They never fight,' I said. 'Not with their claws, anyway. They put stink on their tails instead. And the lemur with the most stinky tail wins.'

'Interesting,' she said, in a way that clearly meant: *'I'm leaving now.'*

Then she left.

I think I might be in love.

Saturday 25 October

No school drop-off today, so I spent the day working on Oscar. Do you know how to make a soft toy? Just in case you want to work in Father Christmas's workshop one day, let me tell you.

1. Make sure you have two pieces the right shape, then sew them together, but do it so that the fur is on the inside. Don't sew it all the way up and make sure you leave a little gap.

2. Use a special stick with a hook on it, so that you can pull the inside out. (This is especially useful if you're making a very small lemur.) Now the fur is on the outside, and the sewed bits are on the inside, which is exactly where you want them to be.

3. Use the stick (or your finger) to push in little bits of stuffing until the toy takes shape.

4. Sew on the tail. Obviously for Oscar that's quite a big job.

5. Sew on the eyes and nose.

When the replacement Oscar was finished, I felt really pleased with him.

But proud as I was, nothing prepared me for Plum's reaction. She squealed!

'Oscar!' she cried. 'You're back!'

'What *is* that?' asked my older sister, Bay, who — along with my older brother, Bo — had called in for supper. They're both over 180 years old and have jobs (which they love to remind me about). They've moved out now, so we only ever see them at weekends.

'My toy lemur,' said Plum proudly. 'I lost him, so Tog made me another one.'

'A lemur?' asked Bo, as he dipped a hunk of bread into the pot that was simmering on the stove. 'Looks more like a squashed racoon. Or a badger that's been run over.'

'Or a zebra,' added Bay. 'That's had cosmetic surgery.'

'Speaking of toys,' said Bo. 'Any reply from Father Christmas?'

I shook my head.

'Shame,' said Bay.

'You applied the day you left school, right?' pressed Bo.

'And that was, what? A year ago?' asked Bay.

I nodded.

'Don't take it to heart,' said Bay.

'It was a bit of a long shot,' agreed Bo.

Bay put her arm around my shoulders, which for

some reason made me feel worse. 'Trust me,' she said. 'We know how you feel. We felt like total losers until we got our jobs at the ice rink.'

Sunday 26 October

Took Leaf, Twig, Pin, Plum and Socks to the ice rink. It was very busy. I've been teaching Plum to skate, and she's slowly getting more confident.

There was a big sign by the hot chocolate stand saying: *Boxing Day Pairs Competition. Entry: 5 acorns per couple*. I wonder if I should enter, just in case I can find someone to skate with? Though if I didn't win, it would be a waste of money, and at the moment every acorn I get comes from my parents.

Spotted a girl in the crowd with red hair. Thought for a moment it might be the girl from the craft shop, but it wasn't.

Monday 27 October

Nothing interesting happened.

Tuesday 28 October

My life is so boring.

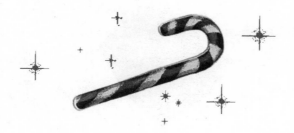

Wednesday 29 October

Something happened today that really cheered
me up.

While I was waiting at the school gates, a
little girl sidled up to me.

'Are you Plum's brother?' she asked.

I said that I was.

'Would you make a lemur for me too?'

I smiled a huge smile and said that I definitely would.

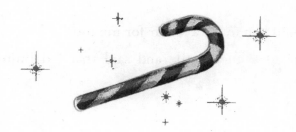

Thursday 30 October

Two more orders for lemurs from two boys in Plum's class.

Friday 31 October

Plum's entire class have ordered lemurs.
I'm really not sure why! I mean, they must already have soft toys of their own. But I guess they are the ordinary kind, where the eyes are straight and the stuffing is even. My lemurs are a bit more *individual*.

Or as Bo and Bay might say, *weird-looking*.

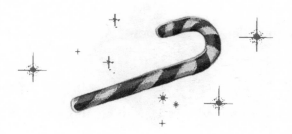

Saturday 1 November

I saw the girl with red hair today!

It was at the craft shop when I was buying more lemur supplies. She tapped me on the shoulder as I was tugging at a giant roll of fur.

'They have a matriarchal society,' she said.

For a moment I wasn't sure what she was talking about.

'Lemurs. They live in troops. And the females are in charge.'

'Yes!' I said, thrilled that I had someone to share my lemur knowledge with. 'The females eat and drink first. Before the males, that is.'

'So how come you're making lemurs?'

I explained about Plum, and Oscar, and the kids in Plum's class. When I had finished, she nodded and looked thoughtful.

'I'm applying to be a Christmas Elf,' she said. 'Maybe you should too?'

'I tried,' I said. 'But I didn't get a reply.'

'Really?' she said. 'That's strange. Maybe your letter got lost?

I was about to say that, yes, maybe it had, when the

roll of fur finally came loose and the entire display fell down on top of me. By the time I'd fought my way out, she was gone.

Friday 7 November

Phew. There's been no time to write my diary this week because I've spent every spare minute making thirty-seven lemurs. I took them with me at pick-up time and Plum's entire class came crowding around me, laughing and clapping with joy. I handed out the lemurs, and they all started to play with them straight away, naming them, cuddling them and making them talk to each other. I felt so happy, like my life finally had a purpose.

This must be what it's like to be Father Christmas! Except, of course, that he never sticks around for children to say 'thank you'. He just leaves the toys and creeps away without anyone seeing him. Which sort of makes it all the more impressive, I think – he doesn't need the praise.

Even if I can't be a Christmas Elf, at least I can make children happy by making them presents the rest of the year. Although I'm not sure I'll have enough acorns to buy all the materials at this rate.

Saturday 8 November

Very tired. Slept.

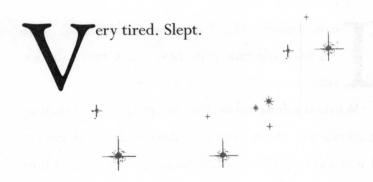

Sunday 9 November

I can't believe what happened today.

I took the four little ones with me to the ice rink.

While teaching them, I've got quite good at skating backwards, which I'm very pleased about. Anyway, I was showing off my skills to Leaf, Twig, Pin, Plum and Socks when a small crowd began to form. They started to whoop and cheer, and the more noise they made, the more I showed off.

I was just beginning to get tired, when who should appear but the girl with red hair! The whole crowd started to clap in unison, and she joined in.

Excited, I decided to skate in smaller and smaller circles. Which was when things went a bit wrong. I tried to finish with a spin, but I haven't really learned how to do that yet, so I slipped and ended up spinning on my bottom instead. But no one seemed to mind – they all just carried on clapping.

Exhausted, I clambered to my feet and took a deep bow. Which was when I realised they weren't looking at me at all, but at someone behind me . . .

I turned to see an athletic figure dressed in a purple sparkly suit, with lightning bolts on the arms, spinning faster and faster in a dazzling pirouette! It was him they had been watching, not me!

He came to a dramatic halt in a spray of ice, the crowd burst into applause, and the girl with red hair rushed straight past me and into his arms.

'Max!' she cried.

Of course! Now I recognised him. It was Max Grimmsson, Grimm Grimmsson's son. I guess that makes him Max Grimmssonsson.

'Holly!' he replied.

Oh well. At least I now know her name.

Monday 10 November

Feeling pretty miserable, so no diary today.

Tuesday 11 November

r today.

Wednesday 12 November

r today.

Thursday 13 November

Something incredible has happened.

I was upstairs in my room after dinner, lying on the top bunk, staring at the ceiling, when I heard voices downstairs. The longer I listened, the more familiar one of the voices sounded. Deep, rich, jolly and serious, all at the same time.

It couldn't be . . . could it?

I rushed downstairs. My mother had collapsed on to a chair, while my father was pressing a cold flannel to her forehead.

'Mum! Are you okay?'

'Fur Griz . . . Fur Griz . . .'

'Father Christmas,' my father explained. 'She just opened the door to Father Christmas!'

'What?'

I ran outside, but he had gone.

My mother struggled to catch her breath. 'Here . . .' she managed, holding out a letter. 'It's for you.'

I took it from her in a dream.

*Tog Harket is invited to attend the
Christmas Elf training course at Father
Christmas's workshop, Christmas Place
at 9 a.m., Monday 17 November.*

That's in four days' time!

Father Christmas must have got my application after all!

Friday 14 November

Couldn't sleep last night, I was so excited.

I decided to practise the route to Christmas Place, ready for Monday. So I crept down the ladder from the top bunk, got dressed and snuck outside.

Not that I really needed much practice. Ever

since I was tiny, I had known that was where Father Christmas had his workshop, and ever since I was only slightly more than tiny, I had been sneaking up to the gates for a peek inside, imagining what it must be like to be a Christmas Elf.

There was a bright moon and the snow squeaked when I walked. I tiptoed through the lanes to the school gates, then turned right on Reindeer Way and crunched my way up to the top of the hill.

Peering between the bars of a huge iron gate, I saw the old shoe factory on the left. The sleigh was inside, lit up like an exhibit in a museum. It looked so beautiful, with its gleaming red, green and gold paint, plush leather seats and cosy fur blankets.

Beyond it was Christmas House, which – like

I would soon be walking through those gates!

the rest of Christmas Place — once belonged to Max Grimmsson's father, Grimm Grimmsson, the notorious elfin shoemaker. The factory had closed down after it was discovered that he had been stealing money from his workers.

A warm, happy feeling filled me from my boots to my earmuffs; I couldn't believe it was really possible that soon I would be walking through these gates to begin my training!

I was turning to head home, when a man dressed in red came running out of nowhere, threw open the gate and crashed straight into me. He was carrying a sack full of toys that spilled out all over the cobbles.

'Oi!' he barked. 'What are you doing, blocking the exit like that?'

I gasped. *It couldn't be.* Could it?

'Father Christmas?' A surge of excitement rushed through me. Suddenly I could hardly remember how to speak, breathe, or even stand. 'It's me, Tog,' I blurted.

He grunted and started picking up the toys.

'Here,' I spluttered, 'let me help you.'

The last toy was a games console, and we both reached for it at the same time. Father Christmas's hand was bare, and on it was a tiny tattoo of criss-crossed candy canes. *Strange*, I thought to myself. *Father Christmas has a tattoo!*

'See you on Monday,' I said eagerly.

'Monday?' he mumbled, looking at me a bit shiftily.

'When I start my training.' I suddenly felt shy.

'Thank you so much, Father Christmas. I got my invitation yesterday. You never know — one day I might make Elf of the Year.'

'Oh yes,' said Father Christmas quickly. 'Indeed you might. See you on Monday.'

It was fairly obvious he hadn't the slightest idea what I was talking about, even though he'd personally delivered my invitation. I suppose he's got a lot on his mind with Christmas coming up.

I think he sensed my disappointment, though, because he suddenly let loose a cheery 'Ho ho ho!' that sounded a bit strangled to me.

Then he set his hat straight, slung his sack over his shoulder, and ran off into the night.

Saturday 15 November

Practised the route to Christmas Place again just in case there are any new roadworks or diversions I need to be aware of.

Sunday 16 November

And again, in case a rogue snowdrift blocks a key alleyway.

Monday 17 November

Yay! My first day of training to become a Christmas Elf!

I dropped Leaf, Twig, Pin and Plum off early at school, and headed up to Christmas Place. Unfortunately a delivery sleigh had shed its load of cabbages on The Broad Way, so I was a teensy bit late. Steinar, the Right-Hand Elf, was outside the gate, waiting to meet me.

'Tog Harket, I presume?'

'Call me Tog,' I said, trying to keep my cool. Inside, of course, I was boiling with excitement.

'I was about to give up on you. The other students are already inside. Stand still, please.'

He pointed a little hand-held machine at my forehead. It bleeped and he checked the reading.

'Hmm. That's strange.'

He took a second measurement, then a third, and frowned. 'I think my Spirit Gauge is playing up. It's what we use to measure Christmas Spirit. Can't have a Christmas Elf without Christmas Spirit, can we? No. Never mind, time's a-ticking.

Let's go and join the others.'

Inside the front door was an enormous reception hall, where lots of important-looking elves were rushing around looking very busy indeed. Steinar escorted me to a large desk, where a snooty Reception Elf gave me a security pass. Then we went to a large metal door, where an even snootier Security Elf checked my rucksack. The Security Elf pushed a button and the door slid open.

Beyond it was a tunnel, and Steinar marched ahead.

Cantering candy canes! I thought. *Christmas House goes right back into the mountain!*

'Keep up!' called Steinar, disappearing round a corner.

I scurried after him, as the tunnel swerved left and right.

We passed an open doorway.

'Mission Control,' he announced, without breaking stride.

I peeked into an enormous cavern filled with row after row of whispering Tech Elves. There was a giant map of the world on the wall, covered with tiny flashing red and green lights.

'What happens in there?' I asked excitedly, once I had caught up with Steinar again.

'That's where we track Father Christmas round the world on Christmas night.'

I had a hundred questions, but before I could ask them, we passed another doorway.

'Candy Caves,' he declared.

At the end of a short passageway I saw a large service lift clanking to a halt, the doors sliding open to reveal a dozen or so Mining Elves. They were all chattering excitedly and their helmets were dusted with sherbet. I guessed they must be finishing their shift.

By the time I looked back at Steinar, he had gone. I had to run to keep up.

'Mail train,' he shouted, as he passed a brick archway. Beyond it was a long railway platform, where Postal Elves were unloading mail bags from an enormous steam train.

Once again, I had to run to keep up.

'Watch your backs!' called an urgent voice. A

caged trolley full of brand-new toys was trundling towards us.

'Morning, Ola!' called Steinar.

The trolley swerved, and Father Christmas's Left-Hand Elf emerged from behind it. For a second, I thought he recognised me, which was impossible, because I had only ever met him once, and that was in a dream. All of the elves in the Arctic Hills knew who Ola and Steinar were – they had the most important jobs in Elf Land, but I was just a Trainee Christmas Elf.

'First load of the day,' he grunted. 'And who's this, then?'

Steinar introduced me.

'A pleasure to meet you, Tog,' growled Ola, shaking

me by the hand. I saw that he had a tattoo of criss-crossed candy canes on his hand too. 'Now if you'll kindly step aside, I'm on my way to the warehouse.'

Then he put his weight behind the trolley and pushed past us.

'Does everyone here have one of those tattoos?' I asked, as we hurried on.

Steinar looked at me quizzically.

'Of criss-crossed candy canes,' I explained.

Steinar glanced in Ola's direction, and smiled. 'That's a prison tattoo. You'll see plenty of those around here. Father Christmas is a firm believer in Second Chances. Everyone's welcome, even ex-prisoners, so long as they pass their training.'

I was about to ask whether the candy cane tattoo

on Father Christmas's hand meant *he* had been to prison, too, when Steinar pulled me to a halt.

'And this . . .' Steinar turned to face me, and a tiny smile of pride curled at his lips. 'This is the workshop.'

He pushed his way through, and I scurried after him.

North Pole Radio was playing at full volume, and the air was thick with hammering, drilling and sawing. The smell of fresh paint filled my nostrils, mixed with the scent of wood shavings and the tang of fresh-cut metal. I took a deep breath, as if I was taking a lungful of fresh air in the Arctic Hills.

'Keep up!' called Steinar, as we passed bench

The room was filled with every toy you could think of

after bench of green-jacketed Toymaking Elves. One was packaging an action figure; another was testing bubble mixture; yet another was checking the tension on a catapult. Everywhere I looked I saw masters at work: pasting labels on miniature cans of baked beans, sewing fluffy sprouts, tacking pink fluff on to the tails of unicorns, and painting the spots on miniature plastic cows. The room was filled with every single toy you can possibly think of.

For the first time in my life, I felt like I belonged.

'This way,' said Steinar at the end of the aisle, opening a door with a sign on it that said *Training Room*.

I stepped inside. There was a blackboard on the far

wall, and facing it, marooned in a sea of empty work benches, were two lonely figures.

One of them turned and I recognised a familiar face.

'Holly!'

'Tog!' she exclaimed, giving me a big hug. 'You made it!'

'Sorry?' asked the elf next to her. I was disappointed to see it was her skating partner and all-round perfect-pants, Max Grimmsson! 'Who's this?'

'One of the kindest elves I've ever met,' said Holly with a smile. 'He wrote to Poppa, asking to be a Christmas Elf. But his letter went missing – so I asked if he could join us.'

'Poppa?' I asked, a little bit confused.

Max gave me a funny look. 'You know that Holly

is Father Christmas's daughter, right?'

I hadn't known that, and I told Holly all about bumping into him at the gates.

Holly smiled and shook her head. 'I don't think that was Poppa,' she said politely. 'He was in Antwerp yesterday, at a Christmas fair.'

'It was, I promise,' I said earnestly. 'He had this huge sack of presents, and I helped him pick them up.'

Max looked at me strangely, then said quickly, 'So your letter went missing?'

'Seems that way,' I agreed.

'It's very strange,' announced Steinar, and we all turned to look at him. 'Usually these benches are full of elves, eager to learn the secrets of toymaking.

But this year hardly anyone applied. Perhaps their letters got lost like yours did, Tog. Shall we?'

I quickly took a seat at the bench across from Holly and Max.

'Now I understand you would like to become Toymaking Elves, is that right?'

The three of us nodded.

'Very good. Now, as I'm sure you all know, there's a special kind of magic here at Christmas Place which helps us work at lightning speed. That's how we can read millions of letters and make gazillions of toys in the run-up to Christmas.'

We nodded again.

'Well, that same magic means you can learn faster too. By the end of this week you'll be experts

64

in — amongst other things — plastic injection moulding, digital electronics, metal die-casting and extrusion, and advanced packaging: in short, everything you need to know to make every single toy in the world.'

I put my hand up.

'Yes, Tog?'

'When do we get to join the workshop?'

I couldn't wait to finish my training and start making toys for real!

'I'm coming to that. At the end of the week, as a test of the skills you've learned, I'll ask you each to make one of our showstopper toys. If it's satisfactory, you'll join the workshop and start making toys for Christmas. The first letters from children are already arriving, so there's lots to do.'

'And if it's not?' asked Max.

'Not what?'

'Satisfactory.'

Steinar smiled.

'Just make sure it is,' he said.

Wednesday 19 November

I am . . . EXHAUSTED.

I was too tired to write yesterday – there is *so* much you have to learn about making toys.

Where to start? Yesterday morning, I suppose . . .

As soon as we arrived for our second day, Steinar tested us with the Spirit Gauge. He seemed very happy with Holly and Max's readings, but when it came to me it went haywire.

Maybe there's something wrong with me.

After that we learned aeronautics, electro-magnetism, palaeontology and fluid dynamics.

Then we had lunch in the canteen. Unfortunately Max chose a table with only two spaces, so I had to sit on my own.

In the afternoon, we studied classical mechanics, quantum theory and how to make a zip. Making a zip was definitely the most complicated.

Holly got hers a bit snarled up and I tried to help her, but Max said she could manage very well on her own, thank you.

It's like he doesn't want us to be friends.

I think he's worried that if she makes friends with me, she won't be friends with him. But that's silly. We can all be friends together.

I guess he isn't as confident as he looks.

Plus, it can't be easy for him, working in what used to be his dad's factory.

Which brings me to today.

As well as all the other things Steinar explained, we learned something I was very interested in indeed: soft toy construction.

It's pretty much the same method I was using to make all the lemurs, except all the pieces for the toy are designed on a computer, measured precisely and sewn on a machine.

That way every toy you make is exactly the same,

which I think is very clever.

Now I know what I'm going to make as my showstopper: a lemur.

But this one is going to be made the correct way!

Holly's making a drone, which is a good choice.

I asked Max what he was going to make, and he said to mind my own business.

Thursday 20 November

Advanced packaging today.

Steinar explained to us that the aim is to make it as difficult as possible to get the toy out of the box, so you have to try and think of as many ways as you can of catching people out.

Some of the best ways are:

1. Make the plastic so thick you need bolt cutters to get into it.
2. Wind little bits of wire around the toy that are impossible to undo.
3. Secure things in place with fiddly plastic screws.

At the end of the day, Steinar asked me to stay behind. He took another reading with his Spirit Gauge, but he still didn't seem very happy with it.

'Sorry,' he said. 'It's still faulty. We're going to have to do this some other time.'

I was about to ask what happens to Trainee Elves who don't have enough Christmas Spirit to work the

Spirit Gauge when Ola, the Left-Hand Elf, marched up and whispered something in Steinar's ear.

'I beg your pardon?' asked Steinar, horrified.

Ola looked at me, and then whispered again.

'A whole sack?'

Ola nodded.

'Leave it with me,' replied Steinar, hurrying off.

'Is something the matter?' I asked.

'Some toys have gone missing,' Steinar called over his shoulder. 'Nothing for you to worry about. I'm sure they'll turn up.'

Friday 21 November

The end of the first week, and today we had to make our showstopper toy.

Things started well enough. I designed my lemur on the computer, then made my cookie-cutter pieces. I used the same super-soft fur that I use for my own lemurs, and the same coloured eyes.

Then I used the sewing machine to stitch it all together.

But somehow it just didn't look the same — like it wasn't alive, or even that friendly.

I still had an hour left, so I decided to scrap it and start again.

So I made a lemur my way. He definitely seemed alive, but he wasn't exactly . . . perfect.

Had I done the right thing? I wasn't sure. But by then it was too late; we had to hand our toys in to Ola.

'Very good,' he said, as he

examined Holly's drone. 'What's the range?'

'Ten kilometres,' answered Holly, 'and you can cloak it.'

'Impressive. May I?'

Holly handed him the controls, and Ola flew the drone three times around the room. Then he flicked a switch and it disappeared! Looking around the room for it, I suddenly felt it hit me on the back of the head.

'Well, that's a pass. And what about you, Max?'

'I made a next-generation VR headset,' said Max. 'And as a bit of fun, I designed some games for it.'

'What sort of games?'

'There's a dancing one. And a motor-racing one. And an ice-skating one. You can actually play that with a partner,' said Max, and I saw him catch Holly's eye.

'Ice skating?'

'Holly and I have entered the Boxing Day Pairs Competition,' explained Max. 'And I thought this might be a good way of practising.'

My insides deflated like a burst balloon when he said that. I realised that deep down, even though we had never skated together and I had only ever spoken to her three times, I'd hoped that Holly would enter the Boxing Day Pairs Competition with me.

'Ingenious,' said Ola. 'You two seem to have a lot in common. And, Tog, what's this?'

'A lemur,' I said.

Max stifled a giggle.

'A lemur?' Ola lifted it up for a closer look.

I nodded.

'Not a honey badger with indigestion? Or a panda

who's swallowed a wasp?'

I shook my head. I had to admit, next to Max's VR headset and Holly's fixed-wing drone, my lemur looked a little bit . . . well . . . home-made.

'Max and Holly, welcome to the Toymaking workshop,' said Ola.

He looked at me and paused, as if he wanted to be as tactful as possible.

'Tog . . .'

I looked at him hopefully.

'How do you feel about reindeer?'

Saturday 22 November

S o, what I've learned is that there's more than one kind of Christmas Elf. The Toymaking Elves are the ones everyone's heard of, but there are lots of others that are just as important.

At least, that's what Ola said.

After we had all made our toys, he and Steinar had a long chat with me, and together we decided that, although I wanted to be a Toymaking Elf, maybe I'd be better off as a Reindeer Elf. It's a bit of a shame, but at least I get to be out in the fresh air, and I *do* love animals.

So that's where I am today. In the reindeer stables.

My job is to muck them all out. Today I mucked out Dasher and Dancer.

Basically you fork all the poo into a barrow, then you tip the barrow into a slurry pit. Then you hose down the stall, leave it to dry, then put down fresh straw.

It's very satisfying, and just as important as making toys. Honest.

Tuesday 25 November

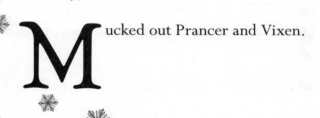

Mucked out Prancer and Vixen.

Wednesday 26 November

Mucked out Comet and Cupid.

Thursday 27 November

Mucked out Donner and Blitzen.

Friday 28 November

Mucked out Rudolph.

I think he might have a bad tummy because . . . I don't know how to put this nicely . . . the floor of his stable is a bit liquid.

I was just sloshing the last shovelful of slimy manure into the barrow when its front wheel collapsed, pouring its entire contents into my wellingtons.

'Now that's unlucky,' said a friendly voice.

I looked around, but all I could see was an old reindeer with a red nose.

'There's a tap over there. You can wash your boots out. Sorry about the stall – had a bit of a funny tummy last night.'

It was Rudolph, and his lips were moving!

'Err . . . thanks,' I said, once I had recovered from the shock. 'Sorry, I've never met a talking reindeer.'

Rudolph bared his teeth, pulling his mouth up at the sides, which I guess was his attempt at a smile.

'If it's any consolation,' he said, 'neither have I. I seem to be the only one. Here, watch this.'

He turned to face the neighbouring stall.

'How's the hay today, Blitzen?'

I followed his gaze to where Blitzen was

staring blankly into space.

'See? Not a word. I've tried everything: sport, politics, celebrity gossip. Not a dicky bird. I find it very difficult. You see, being *heard* is one of my things.'

Blitzen snorted and shook his antlers.

'I think he can hear,' I said. 'He just can't reply.'

There was a long pause, while Rudolph looked at me, then at Blitzen, then at me again.

'You think?' he asked, with a note of genuine surprise.

I kicked off my boots and rinsed them under the tap. Then I rinsed my feet and socks. Then I wondered how I was going to dry myself.

'Here,' said Rudolph. 'Use this.' He tugged the

blanket off his back and tossed it over to me.

'Thanks,' I said. 'Well, your stall's clean. Anything else I can do for you?'

'Now you mention it . . . If you could just pass me some of those dry oats from the hopper there? This stuff is a tad damp.'

I did as he asked.

'May I ask one more favour?' he said.

'Anything,' I replied.

'Would you mind standing a bit further away? It's just that you absolutely stink.'

87

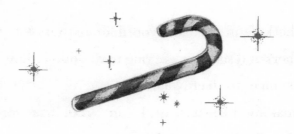

Saturday 29 November

Plum woke me up early. On a Saturday.

'Phew!' she said. 'What's that smell?'

'Sorry,' I answered. 'I didn't have time for a shower last night.'

Leaf, Twig and Pin sat up in their bunks.

'One of my friends wants a lemur!' squeaked Leaf. 'And mine!' said Twig. 'And mine!' said Pin. 'And all the kids in my class you made lemurs for, their brothers and sisters want one too!' added Plum.

It's nice to feel wanted. Even if I can't be a Toymaking Elf, at least I can make toys for the children in the village.

Sunday 30 November

Spent the day making ninety-four lemurs.

'So? What news from Christmas House?' asked Bay, when she and Bo came by for lunch.

'It's really exciting,' I said. 'I'm training to be a Reindeer Elf.'

Bo and Bay smiled at each other.

'I thought you wanted to make toys?' asked Bo.

'I used to,' I said. 'But I think this is more me.'

'So what sort of thing does a Reindeer Elf do?' asked Bo.

'Where do I start?' I said. 'Grooming. Waxing harnesses. Exercising.'

'Anything else?' asked Bay.

'Absolutely,' I replied. 'Nutrition. Hoof care. Dressage. Loads of stuff.'

'What about mucking out?'

'Yes,' I said slowly. 'There's a little bit of that too.'

'Because my friend Star who works in the Clementine Forest says you spend all day shovelling poo.'

I was about to say that without the slurry from

the reindeer to fertilise the clementine trees, there wouldn't even be a Clementine Forest, but I thought better of it.

Monday 1 December

Disaster.

When I arrived at work this morning there was a large crowd outside the reindeer stables, staring up at a hole in the roof.

'What's happened?' I asked.

'Some Trainee Elf was mucking out the reindeer, and he gave Rudolph magic oats,' said a Postal Elf.

93

'Poor Rudolph shot up like a rocket. He's been up there all weekend.'

I glanced over at the hopper I had fed Rudolph from. The oats were sparkly. Next to it was another hopper, with ordinary oats in it. How had I not noticed that before?

I stopped by Mission Control. There was a large crowd of elves watching the screen, as a red blinking light tracked across Greenland.

'There he goes,' said an elf with a buzz cut. 'Looks like he's circling the North Pole.'

'Trying to burn off some steam,' said another.

I decided to leave everyone to it, and went to muck out Dasher and Dancer.

Ola was waiting for me.

'You've heard about Rudolph?'

'I'm really sorry,' I said.

'He's done three thousand miles in the last half hour and he's been going round in circles all weekend!'

'I know. I think I gave him magic oats by mistake.'

Ola's face clouded with anger.

'Tog! What were you thinking?'

'It was an accident,' I blurted. 'He asked me for them and I didn't see the sparkly bits.'

There was a long pause while Ola tried to get the better of his temper. When he finally spoke, his words were curt and gruff.

'Being a Christmas Elf . . . it's not for everyone.'

'It's one mistake,' I protested. 'You can't fire me for one mistake!'

'When it's a mistake this big –' he shrugged – 'I'm afraid I can.'

Tuesday 2 December

Don't really feel like writing my diary today.

Wednesday 3 December

r today.

Thursday 4 December

r today.

Friday 5 December

I've even made Socks depressed. He's just curled up in his basket with his back to everyone.

Saturday 6 December

There were three more kids at the door this morning, wanting me to make lemurs.

I told them I've retired.

'Why?' they asked.

'Because I'm not a Christmas Elf,' I said. 'I've been fooling myself. I just don't have what it takes.'

Then I went back to bed.

Then Twig and Plum woke me up.

'Tog, get up! You have to come!'

'Come where?'

'Christmas Place.'

'It's Saturday,' I replied. 'Plus, they fired me, remember?'

'There's a demonstration! About you! Every young elf in the village is there!'

As we got to the top of the hill we could hear voices chanting:

'Take Tog Back! Take Tog Back!'

Outside Christmas Place there was a huge crowd of young elves, with some baby elves as young as fifty. Ola was at the gates, trying to reason with them, but all the elves just booed him.

102

'Tog deserves a second chance!' shouted one.

'Lemur-lovers unite!' bawled another.

'Tog!' hissed Plum. 'You're famous!'

Sunday 7 December

Well, today has been the strangest in my entire one hundred and sixty years, and that includes the time I ate some leftover turkey three weeks after Christmas and got food poisoning.

It started when Steinar called at our house.

When I asked him what he was doing there, he

said Father Christmas wanted to see me.

'But I messed up,' I said. 'Ola fired me for giving Rudolph magic oats.'

'I know,' said Steinar. 'But Father Christmas believes in second chances.'

He had a husky sled waiting and we drove out of the town, through the forest, all the way to Father Christmas's lodge.

There was a huge Christmas tree in the front garden, covered in brightly coloured lights.

Steinar tied up the huskies and led me inside. 'Now *don't* embarrass me, Tog,' he hissed, as we entered a hallway glowing with a roaring fire, with garlands of holly wrapped around the banisters, draped over the mantelpiece and hanging from the ceiling.

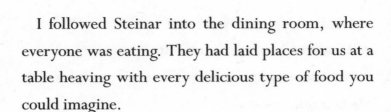

I followed Steinar into the dining room, where everyone was eating. They had laid places for us at a table heaving with every delicious type of food you could imagine.

'Hi, Tog. Come and get some pie before I eat it all!' called a cheerful voice.

It was Holly, sitting in the middle of her nine older brothers and seven older sisters, some of whom I recognised from Christmas Place. Then I spotted Max smirking at me from behind an enormous chicken leg and my excitement quickly disappeared. Mrs Christmas served me a huge slice of steaming pie and vegetables, and told me to call her Gerda.

There was lots of laughter, and after lunch we

stood around the fire with cups of mead and sang Christmas carols.

Later on, Father Christmas invited me to his study. He seemed different to when I bumped into him at the gates that time – much less stressed. I told him so, but he didn't seem to know what I was talking about. I guess there are a lot of elves at the workshop and it's hard for him to keep track.

He held up one of my lemurs.

'Do you know who this belongs to?'

I shook my head. Father Christmas gestured towards a comfortable-looking chair in front of his desk, and I sat down.

'My grandson Sprig. He goes to the same school as your sister Plum. He says you made it for him.'

I nodded.

'And do you know what else he said?'

I shook my head.

'He said it's his favourite toy.'

Father Christmas beamed at me, and as nervous as I was, I couldn't help but grin back.

There was a knock at the door and Steinar entered, carrying a large cardboard box.

'The fairy dust has arrived,' he announced, and he opened the box to reveal a tiny jar with a cork stopper, full of sparkly powder.

'What's that?' I asked.

Father Christmas and Steinar looked at one another, as if they were deciding whether or not to share an important secret.

'Sometimes,' said Father Christmas in a low voice, 'when I try to deliver the presents, the children aren't quite asleep. So I take a tiny pinch of this and . . .'

He mimed putting a pinch of dust in his hand, then blew it towards me. I felt his breath on my face, and it smelled of sugarplums.

'It sends them into a deep, deep sleep.'

I wanted to pinch myself. Was Father Christmas really sharing his secrets with me, Tog Harket of the East Village? What would Leaf, Twig, Pin and Plum think of this? Let alone my mother and father, and Bay and Bo?

'On the subject of deep sleep, Tog,' said Steinar, 'I feel that's what I must have been in, ever since I met you. I owe you an apology. I've taken your Christmas

Spirit reading three times, and each time it's been so high that I thought my Spirit Gauge was broken. I realise now those readings were correct; it was me that was at fault. You have more Christmas Spirit than everyone else in Christmas Place put together!'

'Now, now,' said Father Christmas. 'Let's not go overboard. The point is, Tog, perfection in presents is important. That's why we train our elves to make every toy the same. No one wants a situation where two children ask for bicycles, and one bicycle is better than the other. But there's an exception. An exception I think you understand better than anyone.'

He walked out from behind his desk and sat next to me on the arm of the chair.

'Every child in the world has One Special Toy. A toy that becomes a friend. Where they go, it goes. Every time they go to sleep, they want it next to them. If it gets lost, their parents will move heaven and earth to find it for them, it's that important.'

He put his hand on my shoulder.

'That toy can be many things. It can be a teddy bear, a rabbit, a dog . . . even a blanket.'

He held Sprig's lemur up in front of us. Its lopsided mouth seemed to be grinning.

'Or one of your lemurs.'

He pushed Sprig's lemur into my chest. I couldn't really see how its wonky eyes and slightly ragged tail were special, but I didn't want to contradict Father Christmas, so I nodded along.

'Every other kind of toy we make has to be perfect. But not the special toys. They have to be one of a kind. Few elves can make them. And you . . .'

He sat back down behind his desk and looked me squarely in the eye.

'You are one of those elves.'

The special toys have to be one-of-a-kind

Monday 8 December

I made it!

I'm a Toymaking Elf!

I've got my own bench and everything, right next to Max and Holly.

I'm making lemurs for Christmas!

I don't think I've ever been so happy in my entire life.

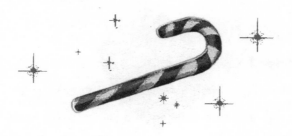

Tuesday 9 December

I made 564 lemurs today.

Max is much nicer to me these days. At lunchtime today he let me play the ice-skating game on his VR headset.

He's asked me to go skating with him and Holly next weekend.

Maybe I was wrong about him.

I'm not sure Ola is happy that I'm back in the workshop. I saw him whispering to Steinar, and afterwards they both looked really worried.

Tomorrow I'm going to try extra hard with my lemurs. Maybe then they'll see that Father Christmas was right to give me a second chance.

116

Wednesday 10 December

Made 565 lemurs. That's a new personal best.

Thursday 11 December

Made 563 lemurs. Real off-day.

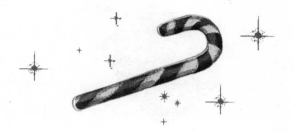

Friday 12 December

I made 565 lemurs. I would have made 566 or possibly even 567, but this morning Ola and Steinar called a surprise meeting for all the Toymaking Elves, which took up a bit of time.

'I want to talk to you all about security,' said Steinar. Slowly, the hammering, sawing and filing stopped as one by one all the Toymaking Elves realised they were being spoken to.

'I don't know how to say this. But Steinar and I have counted the toys in the warehouse and some of them are missing.'

A loud gasp rang around the room.

'It could be a mistake,' said Steinar. 'It's always possible that we've miscounted, or that there's a sackful of toys somewhere, fallen behind a workbench, perhaps, or . . .'

He looked at Ola.

'We've been concerned about this for a while, but I really can't think of how it could have happened. Unless . . .'

He seemed unwilling to say the words that

were forming on his lips.

'. . . someone stole them.'

The room burst into excited chatter, as elf turned to elf in disbelief.

'I know, I know,' said Ola. 'It's hard to imagine. But we have to face the possibility that somewhere here in Christmas Place . . . is a thief. So from now on I want each and every one of you to keep your eyes and ears open. And if any of you sees anything out of the ordinary, please report to me.'

Saturday 13 December

Went skating with Max and Holly. They showed me their routine for the Boxing Day Pairs Competition. It's really good, though a lot of it involves Holly watching while Max does pirouettes.

Max asked me what I thought of it, and I said

maybe Holly should do some pirouettes herself.

For a minute he looked quite cross. Then he smiled and he said he thought that was a really good suggestion.

'Tell you what, Tog,' he said. 'You should be our coach.'

I said maybe Max should dip Holly at the end.

They didn't understand, so I dipped Holly to demonstrate.

Unfortunately when I was dipping her my ears went really hot and I got a nosebleed.

Luckily Max made it stop by putting snow down the back of my tunic. Afterwards we went for hot chocolates, and Holly said that Father Christmas is really worried about the toys going missing.

Max said it was probably just a misunderstanding, and I agreed with him. I mean, there's no way any of the elves at the workshop would ever be involved in stealing.

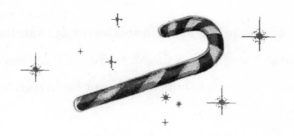

Sunday 14 December

O h wow.

It's early.

I mean, really early.

In fact, it's the middle of the night.

But I just remembered something.

When Steinar took me to Father Christmas's lodge,

125

and Father Christmas put his hand on my shoulder . . .

HE DIDN'T HAVE A CANDY CANE TATTOO.

So that must mean that the night I went to Christmas Place . . .

That Father Christmas was a fake!

What if he's the thief everyone's looking for?

Monday 15 December

First thing this morning, I went to tell Ola. The mail train had just come in, and he was working on the platform, supervising the Postal Elves.

I told him the whole story, about how a fake Father Christmas had bumped into me, and he had been carrying lots of toys. And that I knew he was fake because he had criss-crossed candy canes tattooed on his hand!

Ola put his hands behind his back, and leaned forward, as if he was listening very carefully. He told me not to tell anyone. 'This could be the breakthrough we've been hoping for,' he said. 'Well done, Tog. Well done.'

Tuesday 16 December

I made 567 lemurs. Another personal best!

Thursday 18 December

I'm in a police cell!

There's been a terrible mistake.

I have to get my thoughts in order. And then I have to figure out how I'm going to get out of here.

The day started really well. The thought of Christmas being just round the corner gave me lots of Christmas Spirit, and by hometime I'd made 569 lemurs, the most I've ever made in one day.

Then something awful happened.

Usually we all file out of the tunnel, through the security gate, and go home. But when we reached the reception area there was a line of Security Elves searching everyone's bags.

When the Security Elf opened my rucksack, it was full of lemurs!

'Hallo, hallo,' he said. 'Where did these come from?'

I had no idea.

Ola and Steinar took me into a side room.

'Tog?' asked Steinar. 'What's going on?'

'Nothing,' I said. 'I promise you!'

'Two hundred and fifty-nine lemurs isn't *nothing*,' corrected Ola. 'They're worth a lot of money.'

'But they're not mine!' I protested. 'I mean, they are – I made them – but someone else must have put them in there!'

'A fake Father Christmas, perhaps?' asked Ola with a sneer. 'No wonder you told me that crackpot story. You were trying to throw us off the scent. When all along the toy thief was *you*.'

He prodded me so hard in the chest that the bell on the end of my hat jingled. Then they bundled me off in a police sled and now I'm here, waiting to be questioned.

What am I going to do?

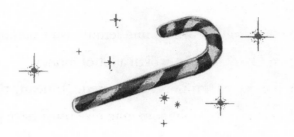

Friday 19 December

I'm so tired. I'm still at the police station. Elf Detectives have been asking me questions all day, and no one seems to believe me.

I'm not allowed to see anyone — not even my parents.

They say I'm going to be charged with Toy Stealing.

Saturday 20 December

S pent the day at Thistledown Magistrate's
  Court.

I had to wait for ages for the judge to hear
my case. There were lots of dodgy-looking elves
milling around, waiting too.

Eventually I was called up into the courtroom.
There was a red-faced elf in the dock and, listening

to the conversation, it seemed like he had been caught drunk in charge of a sleigh.

'How do you plead?' asked the magistrate. She was wearing a long powdered wig.

'Guilty, Your Worship,' said the red-faced elf. 'I am wracked with shame. And on my life, not so much as a drop of mead shall pass my lips again.'

'Very well,' came the reply. 'We look favourably on those who save the court's time by pleading guilty. Three weeks' litter duty at the ice rink.'

'Your Worship's mercy is humbling. You shall not see me again, I promise,' intoned the red-faced elf.

As he passed me, he took a nip from a hip flask and gave me a cheeky wink.

A Police Elf took me by the arm and I found myself in the dock, facing the magistrate.

'Tog Harket, you are charged with the theft of two hundred and fifty-nine lemurs from Father Christmas's workshop.'

There was a sharp intake of breath from the clerk of the court, as if she had never heard anything so scandalous.

'How do you plead?'

'Innocent,' I blurted.

'What?'

'It wasn't me!'

The magistrate tutted, and shook her head.

'Please don't waste our time, Mr Harket,' she said. 'I've read the statements. You were caught red-handed. Show me that you're sorry, and I'll go easy on you.'

'It's not fair!' I protested. 'I didn't do it, I promise.'

There was a long pause.

'Tog Harket, you will be remanded until such a time as you may face trial in court.'

Sunday 21 December

I'm at Cloudberry Maximum Security Prison! It's like a fortress.

I'm in D Wing, where they keep the hardened criminals. I'm sharing my cell with an elf called Pippin who's doing six weeks for flying a kite in a public park.

I've met some of the other inmates too. Just like Steinar said, they all had candy cane tattoos.

Some of them have committed horrific crimes. Snarler threw hedge clippings into his neighbour's garden. Baldra sold hawthorn berries to a group of elderly elves, claiming they were rosehips. And Hod went ziplining in a built-up area.

I've got to get out of here.

Fake Father Christmas is behind all this, I'm sure of it. I bet he's the one who put lemurs in my rucksack.

Somehow I have to catch him, and prove my innocence.

But how? I'm not allowed visitors, so I can't get a message to anyone. And Cloudberry is legendary. In its entire six thousand years, no one has ever escaped.

An elf called Pickle who's in for Hairdressing Without a Licence offered to give me a tattoo, but I said, 'No, thank you.'

When he pressed me, I said I was going to escape and prove my innocence.

He laughed so much he said his extensions hurt.

I felt quite down after that, so to cheer myself up I used Association Time to visit the prison library. I looked for a book on lemurs, but there weren't any animal books at all. There weren't any toymaking books either, so I ended up in the Biography section.

My eye fell on a familiar face: Grimm Grimmsson. He was beaming out from the cover of a tattered hardback book with the title *On Top of the World —*

How I Became the North Pole's Most Successful Elf Ever.

It was hard to believe that the confident elf in the photograph was the same one who had run away with the shoemakers' pension fund, never to be seen again. And then I thought how sad it must be for Max, not having his father around. No wonder he was a bit difficult sometimes.

I opened the front cover, and in it was a list of the prisoners who had borrowed the book.

One of the names was Ola Handsensen.

Of course! Ola had a candy cane tattoo!

I'd only ever seen it once, the first time I met him, when Steinar was showing me around. But it was definitely there!

Which meant *he* might be Fake Father Christmas!

It was all guesswork, and everyone says I keep getting things wrong.

I needed evidence.

And how could I get any, locked away in my prison cell?

PRISON LIBRARY

Name	Date
Baldra Milkthistle	1 FEB
Ola Handsensen	26 FEB
Miks Lindgren	6 JUN
Karl Munt	14 JUL
Pickles Picklesson	12 AUG
Mags Fakkelborg	23 OCT
Klint Poppleweed	3 DEC

Monday 22 December

Had a really weird dream last night.

I was at the bottom of a very deep well, so deep the top was a tiny circle of light no bigger than an acorn.

There was a rope dangling above me, which I could somehow see in the dark.

It was my only way out.

I put out my hand to take hold of it, but it was a little higher than I thought, so I stood on tiptoes. I jumped and grabbed at it, but my hands clapped shut just short of it.

No matter what I did, the rope would always be beyond my grasp. I was stuck in the well for ever. I started to panic. 'Help!' I screamed. 'Help!'

'Tog! Tog!' called a voice.

It was Pippin, my cellmate.

'Wake up!' he said. 'You're having a bad dream.'

I was on the top bunk, and Pippin was shaking me by the shoulder.

I told him about the well and the rope, and he nodded. 'You need some fresh air,' he said. 'And today's your lucky day. We get to visit the exercise yard.'

The yard was huge, about the size of the ice rink

in the village. It felt wonderful to look up and see the glittering sky. It felt sad, too, because I realised that it might be years before I was free again.

I thought about Leaf, Twig, Pin, Plum and Socks, and how much I missed them. And my mother and father. Even Bay and Bo.

I felt something sting in my eye, and suddenly a tear went rolling down my cheek and burned a hole in the snow.

'Tog,' hissed a familiar voice.

I looked around, but there was no one anywhere near me. Pippin was right across the other side of the yard, trading acorns with Snarler, Baldra and Hod; and the two Guard Elves were chatting by the basketball hoop.

'It's me – Holly!'

I turned around and around. Was I going crazy? There was no one there!

'Over here!'

I looked in the direction that the voice was coming from.

'Look!'

Suddenly Holly's drone uncloaked in front of me, then cloaked again!

I glanced across at the guards, then at Pippin and friends, to check whether they had seen it too. They hadn't.

'Holly! What are you doing here?'

'I know you're innocent!'

'What?' I asked. 'How?'

'This drone. It was recording and it filmed

someone putting the lemurs in your rucksack!'

'No way! Who was it?'

'I don't know! They were dressed like Poppa, but it can't be him because he's away doing an appearance at a shopping centre in Nuneaton.'

'Wait . . . They were dressed like Father Christmas?'

'Yes!'

I told her about the fake Father Christmas I'd bumped into, and how he'd been carrying a sackful of toys.

'It must be the same guy!' hissed Holly.

'That's what I think!' I said.

'But who would do such a thing? Who would have the nerve to dress up as Father Christmas? And where would they get the outfit from? Poppa has the only one.'

'I think it might be Ola!'

'Who?'

'Ola, the Left-Hand Elf!'

'You can't be serious?'

'All right, you lot, back inside!' called a gruff voice. It was one of the Guard Elves. Holly and I didn't have much time.

'Holly, you've got to get me out of here!' I hissed.

'Oi! Tog!' yelled the Guard Elf. He was marching towards me. 'Back inside.'

'I'm not coming!' I said.

'Oh yes, you are,' said the Guard Elf, grinning as he removed what looked like a lasso made of Christmas ribbon from its holster. 'Put your hands in the air.'

I did as I was told.

And then I watched the Guard Elf's mouth fall open as I was lifted slowly up into the air.

'What the . . . ?' spluttered the Guard Elf.

I was holding on to the rails of Holly's cloaked drone. But the Guard Elf didn't know that!

'Gotta fly,' I said, and shot off into the sky.

I've no idea how I managed to hang on. The exercise yard fell away beneath me, then D Wing, then the prison walls. Soon the entire prison was the size of a toy fortress, and I was gliding high above the frozen lake that separated Cloudberry from the twinkling lights of the village.

'Hold on!' said Holly. 'I'm bringing you in.'

'Gotta Fly,' I said, and shot off into the sky

There she was, at the edge of the forest, a tiny red-headed speck in the snow!

I hurtled down and landed beside her. My arms were aching, but I gave her an enormous hug all the same.

'He had a prison tattoo!' I blurted. 'Of criss-crossed candy canes.'

'The fake Father Christmas?'

'Exactly. And I think maybe Ola does too.'

Holly nodded slowly, as if she was remembering something.

'That fits. Daddy met Ola years ago, on a visit to Cloudberry. Ola asked for a job, and Daddy gave him one. Ola worked his way up to Left-Hand Elf.'

'We have to tell Steinar!'

'Not without evidence,' said Holly gravely. 'He'd never believe us.'

'We've got evidence!' I exclaimed. 'Fake Father Christmas had a tattoo. If Ola has one too, that's proof!'

'It's not enough. There are lots of elves with those tattoos. Come on!'

Holly clambered on to the drone.

'Where are we going?' I asked, climbing up behind her.

'To Ola's cabin!'

She wrapped my arms around her waist, activated the control pad, and we took off!

We shot straight up into the air, until we were level with the treetops, then powered forward across the forest. With the ice rink in sight, we veered right, and landed on the roof of Ola's lone wooden cabin.

Holly cloaked the drone, tiptoed along the ridge of the roof, and pulled herself up on to the chimney stack. Of course! It ran in the family. Like all Christmases, she was going to climb down the chimney!

'What are we looking for?' I hissed.

'I don't know,' whispered Holly. 'Evidence. Stolen toys, maybe? There must be something that will prove Ola is the fake Father Christmas.'

And with that she disappeared. I heard a soft thump as she landed in the fireplace.

I have to admit, at that moment I had second thoughts.

The lights were out, admittedly, but what if Ola

was home? What if he was innocent after all? We were trespassing, and I had a feeling that the magistrate wouldn't be any nicer to me a second time round. If this went badly, I could find myself getting a D-Wing tattoo after all . . .

'Tog! Where are you?'

It was Holly, calling up the chimney.

There was nothing for it. I had to follow her.

Clump! My feet landed in a pile of soot, and I found myself staring into the darkness of Ola's cabin.

There was the flash of a match, and Holly lit an oil lamp.

The cabin was bare. Just a bed, a sofa and a stove.

'Quick,' said Holly. 'We don't have much time. Look for anything, anything at all, that might prove

Ola is the fake Father Christmas.'

Holly began opening cupboards, and I did the same. There was a small door in the bedside table, so I checked that too. It was empty. Then I noticed a photo in a frame.

'Holly! Look!'

'What is it?'

'A photo. But it's of Grimm Grimmsson. And Max.'

She marched across the room, took it from me and held it in the light.

'Looks old. Grimm is much younger. And Max only looks a hundred or so here.'

She handed it back to me.

'What's Ola doing with a photo of Grimm

Grimmsson?' I asked.

Holly shrugged. Then her eye caught something in the corner of the room.

'Tog, look. Ola's wardrobe!'

I knew instantly what she was thinking: maybe this was where Ola kept his Fake Father Christmas disguise! I ran over and we each took hold of a handle, opening the two doors wide.

The wardrobe was empty.

'Looking for this?'

We turned round to see Max, holding up a Father Christmas outfit.

Holly and I looked at one another, stunned.

Max inhaled and lifted his free hand, which he clenched tight. Then he opened his fingers and blew!

A cloud of tiny fairy dust sparkles took to the air.

Then everything went dark.

Tuesday 23 December

The first thing I saw when I awoke was my own face, reflected in some sort of see-through screen.

Where was I?

Slowly, my eyes adjusted. I was still in Ola's cabin. My hands and feet were tied with plastic-coated wire, like the sort used to package toys, and so was my waist. I was sitting on a cardboard ledge that had been decorated to look like wood, and the screen in front of me was made of plastic. I was in a display box!

I looked across at Holly. She was fast asleep in a display box just like mine. There was writing on it that read: *100% Genuine Elf on the Shelf*.

We'd been packaged!

And what was that hissing sound?

'I thought you'd be waking up about now.'

I turned to see Max steam-ironing the Fake Father Christmas suit.

'Let us out!' I exclaimed. 'Let us out right now!'

'Sorry, old chum, no can do,' said Max, taking care not to burn the white fur around the cuffs.

We'd been packaged!

'It's better this way, trust me. After all, this is what we do with nosey-parker elves, isn't it? We send them to spy on children.'

'Why are you doing this to us?'

'I've booked a courier to take you to an independent toyshop in Seattle,' said Max, ignoring my question. 'I think that's far enough away. Soon you'll be sitting on some poor unsuspecting child's shelf, and you can spy on them all you want. Because that's what you both are, aren't you? Spies?'

'Max, what's going on? Has Ola got to you somehow? We know he's the one who's been stealing toys.'

Max laughed, as if that was a very funny idea indeed.

'You really have no idea, do you?'

He was right. I hadn't.

Max set the iron down, and looked me straight in the eye.

'Ola's my father.'

Now my mouth fell open.

'What? I thought your father was Grimm Grimmsson?'

'It's called a disguise,' said Max, swooshing the jacket off the ironing board and on to a hanger. 'You should try it sometime. You could dress up as a successful elf, instead of a total loser.'

'Ola Handsensen . . . is Grimm Grimmsson?'

'Ironic, isn't it?' said Max, picking a speck of fluff from the red velvet. 'Everyone thought I had no father. Turns out I have two.'

Could it be true? Grimm Grimmsson had a sharp nose and chin, like a hatchet. Ola looked like an angry polar bear. But now I thought about it, they both had the same eyes. Cold. Grey. Calculating.

Max was now steaming the trousers.

'When my father lost the factory, he was forced to run. Everyone thought he'd abandoned me. But he hadn't. He came back . . . as Ola.'

'So how did he end up in prison?'

Max shrugged. 'Father Christmas loves ex-cons. It's that soppy "second chance" thing of his. So Dad threw a snowball at a Police Elf and refused to apologise. That got him his ticket to D Wing – and eventually a job with Father Christmas.'

'So he could steal toys? It doesn't make sense.'

Max shook his head and smiled. 'This isn't about a few toys. This is about revenge.'

'Revenge for what? I don't understand.'

'Oh, I think you do. I think you understand better than anyone. You of all people know what it's like to be looked down on,' jibed Max. 'Father Christmas took everything from us: our home, our factory, our self-respect. And now he's going to pay.'

Max was now hanging up the trousers: the suit was complete.

'Father Christmas didn't take those things! Your father lost them, through his own greed!'

Holly stirred, and Max glanced across at her. 'Those toys we stole, that was just a test. To see if this —' he smirked, holding up the Fake Father

Christmas suit — 'would convince people that Dad was the real Father Christmas.'

A horrible thought struck me. Was that why Max had befriended Holly — so that he could get closer to Father Christmas?

I watched helplessly as Max uncorked the jar of fairy dust and took a pinch between his finger and thumb.

'We're going to steal Christmas. At nine o'clock tomorrow night, we're going to get on that sleigh, and fly away with every single present. This year, not one single child will get a gift from Father Christmas. They'll never trust him again. And then, once his name is dirt, and all the children in the world are desperate for toys, we'll set up our own online toyshop and sell the lot. Father Christmas will be history and *we'll* make a fortune!' He threw his head back and cackled.

'You can't do this, Max!' I protested. 'Children asked for those toys on their Christmas lists, and we made them specially, with love! You can't just sell them!'

Holly half opened one eye.

'Where am I?' she mumbled.

Max opened the lid of Holly's box, and sprinkled in a pinch of fairy dust. Holly's head lolled forward, and she fell straight back into a deep sleep.

'Sorry, Tog,' said Max cheerily. 'Time's ticking. I need to get you ready for the courier.' He held up two rolls of wrapping paper. 'I've only got these two.

Which do you prefer? Christmas trees, or plain?'

'Christmas trees, please,' I replied.

'Plain it is,' said Max, lifting the lid of my box.

I saw a cloud of sparkles, then everything went dark . . .

Wednesday 24 December

I awoke to a strange clacking sound, as if a pixie was playing a tiny pair of castanets.

It was my teeth chattering.

I was still in the display box, bound tight, and I was freezing.

I tried to see out, but soon realised that my box

had been covered in plain brown paper. I could just about make out a crescent moon through it.

The penny dropped.

I was on Ola's doorstep. And Max was about to steal Christmas!

I *had* to escape.

'Holly? Holly!'

Silence.

'Holly, are you there?'

'Tog!' Holly's muffled voice was faint beside me.

'You okay?'

'Fine. Bit of a headache, but fine.'

I breathed a sigh of relief.

'Okay, great. Next question: are you wearing a watch?'

'Yes!'

'What time is it?'

'Quarter to nine!'

I winced. The whole of Christmas Eve had passed. By now the Delivery Elves would be loading the sleigh, as the exhausted Workshop Elves rushed to finish the last few precious presents!

We had fifteen minutes to get out of our parcels and stop Max from stealing Christmas!

I rattled through everything I knew, though I left out the bit about Max using Holly to get close to Father Christmas. She didn't need to hear that.

'There's only one thing for it!' she said, and then shouted: 'HELP!'

'HELP!' I yelled, joining in.

171

But the only answer was the wind.

And a dog barking.

Wait. It couldn't be?

The dog barked again.

Socks!

I put my fingers in my mouth, rolled back my tongue, and made the special whistle we have for calling Socks. Inside the box it sounded deafening. Would Socks hear it too?

Another bark, louder this time!

'SOCKS!' I bellowed. 'SOCKS!'

I heard footsteps in the nearby snow, and suddenly there was Socks's nose, pressed up against the brown paper.

'Over here!'

It was Plum's voice!

'Plum, it's me – Tog! I'm in this parcel!'

The paper above me ripped in two, and Plum's face appeared, lit by the moonlight.

'Tog! We've been looking everywhere for you! Everyone knows you've escaped from jail – there are sleighs out all over the North Pole searching for you.'

Soon Leaf, Twig and Pin were tearing off Holly's wrapping and mine, and opening up our display boxes.

The only problem now was the fastenings. As everyone knows, they are impossible for any child to open.

Luckily Bo and Bay arrived.

'Don't worry,' reassured Bo. 'We've got this. We're always untangling laces at the ice rink.'

We were free! But there was no time to lose.

'Bay, Bo, Leaf, Twig, Pin, Plum and Socks!' I yelled. 'Thank you all so much. But Holly and I have to go and save Christmas!'

'Be careful,' warned Bay.

'Take Oscar!' piped Plum, holding up her lemur. 'He'll look after you.'

It seemed like the least I could do, so I tucked Oscar in my tunic and vaulted up to the roof. Holly uncloaked the drone, and I hopped on behind her. Then we took off into the night!

We raced over the ice rink, full of young elves skating by torchlight. Then we banked left towards Christmas House. There below us was the sleigh, laden with presents, surrounded by hundreds of

The sleigh was surrounded by cheering Christmas Elves

cheering Christmas Elves.

We dropped like a stone, down, down, down . . .

Then stopped dead behind the sleigh, just a few metres from the cobbles.

Father Christmas was in the driving seat, with his back to us, waving goodbye.

On the back of his hand, between his thumb and index finger, was a tattoo of two criss-crossed candy canes.

'STOP, THIEF!' I bellowed.

But the elves were cheering too loudly to hear me.

'STOP, THIEF!'

Only one elf turned.

It was Max.

He jumped up beside Fake Father Christmas,

and whispered something in his ear. Fake Father Christmas turned and looked at us and I saw Ola's cold grey eyes looking out from behind the beard. He gathered the reins, and with a 'YAH!' the sleigh lurched forward, scattering elves left, right and centre.

'THAT'S NOT FATHER CHRISTMAS!' I barked. 'HE'S A FAKE!'

But it was too late. The reindeer were gathering pace, arcing around the courtyard and up into the night sky!

'So long, suckers!' screeched Max.

'Let's get them!' shouted Holly.

'Wait!' I cried. Seeing the reindeer had reminded me of something: the slurry pit, where all their poo got dumped. 'Head for the stables!' I yelled. 'I've got an idea!'

Holly did as I asked.

'Go as low as you can,' I called. 'I need to dip Oscar's tail in the pit.'

With expert precision, Holly guided us down to the bubbling, putrid surface. I felt bad for Plum, but I had no choice. In went Oscar's tail, then off we flew!

I have never moved so fast as we did on that drone. At least to begin with. No sooner did we have Fake Father Christmas in our sights, than he started to slip away.

'Faster!' I yelled. 'We're losing him!'

'I'm trying! We're running out of battery!'

'How long have we got?'

'I don't know!' yelled Holly. 'Maybe seconds!'

We were inching closer now. Max glanced over his shoulder, his eyes widening as he saw us. His hand disappeared into his jacket pocket, and just in time I realised what he was up to!

'Holly, watch out!'

We swerved sharply, just missing a glittering cloud of sparkles!

Max was throwing fairy dust!

Holly swerved again, as another cloud of dust burst out – and another.

'We've got to get in front of them!'

Her face set with determination, Holly manoeuvred us out from behind the sleigh, and came up alongside it. There was nothing Max could do now; his fairy dust had blown away on the wind. All he could do was watch helplessly as we edged closer.

'Go for it!' shouted Holly, and I grabbed Oscar the lemur by the nose, holding him behind me so that his body stretched out like a streamer, his stinky tail dancing on the wind. Little by little, Holly worked the controls until Oscar's super-whiffy tail was right in front of Ola's nose.

'PHWOOAARRR!' howled Ola.

Ola and Max both recoiled, as the heady scent of rotting reindeer poo filled their nostrils.

'EUUURRGGHH!' wailed Max.

'I'M GOING TO BE SICK!' gasped Ola, letting go of the reins. Presents began to tumble off the back of the sleigh as it pitched and rolled.

'CALL IT OFF! CALL IT OFF!' squealed Max.

I had to get control of the sleigh! 'BRING ME IN CLOSER!' I yelled to Holly.

Oscar's toxic tail snaked back and forth, and Ola and Max retreated, holding their noses. I turned so I was facing backwards, then leaped on to the front of the sleigh!

'WHAT ARE YOU DOING?!' bellowed Ola. 'YOU'RE RUINING EVERYTHING!'

I flicked Oscar's tail into his face, and grabbed the reins.

'Rudolph!' I called into the wind. 'It's me, Tog!'

'Tog! What are you doing here?'

'Saving Christmas! We need to go back to base. That okay with you?'

'One hundred per cent,' called Rudolph. 'Guys!' he bellowed to the other reindeer. 'This is Tog, and he wants us to go back to the workshop. Understand?'

All eight reindeer grunted in unison.

'See?' shouted Rudolph. 'You were right. I speak my truth, and they hear it.'

'Follow me!' called Holly, and she started to bank the drone.

'WAIT!'

It was Max. Both he and Ola had hankies over their noses.

'Come with us, Tog! We'll need a frontman. We can call our shop Tog's Toys. You can sell those whatsits you make, polecats . . .'

'Lemurs,' I corrected.

'Whatever. You'll be famous the world over, and rich beyond your wildest dreams. It's better than going back to the workshop, believe me.'

'Never,' I said.

'Trust me, the second that Father Christmas gets hold of you, you'll be back on D Wing.'

For a split second, I panicked. What if Father Christmas didn't believe me? What if I ended up back in prison?

'No,' I said firmly. 'What you're doing is wrong. And somewhere, deep inside, you know that. Both of you. These toys are going back to Father Christmas, and he's going to make sure that all the children of the world get their presents!'

And with that, I gave Oscar a shake, so that his

pooey tail slapped wetly on both their faces.

'Tog!'

It was Holly! She was flying beside me as we headed back towards the North Pole!

'We did it!' she roared. 'We saved Christmas!'

Thursday 25 December

After that, everything ran like clockwork. Rudolph took us back to Christmas Place, where Holly's dad, the real Father Christmas – having been found knocked out with fairy dust and locked in his study – was waiting with Steinar. The Prison Guard Elves that had been scouring the village for me took no time in arresting

185

The sleigh visited every child, delivering presents

Ola and Max, and Holly and I spent the rest of the evening drinking hot chocolate in the control room as we watched the sleigh visit every child on the Good List, delivering presents.

All in all, one of the better Christmas Eves I've spent.

This morning it was business as usual, watching my younger brothers and sisters open their presents.

'I hope you've thanked your brother,' said Dad.

'You wouldn't have any toys at all if it wasn't for him,' added Mum.

'THANK YOU, TOG!' chorused Leaf, Twig, Pin and Plum.

'Yeah, well done,' grinned Bo.

'Our boss at the ice rink said you can skate for free any time,' offered Bay.

And, of course, I gave Oscar back to Plum, freshly laundered by the Christmas Jumper Elves. Even she had to admit he smelled better than he had for a while.

Then it was a quick dash over to Father Christmas's lodge for the Annual Celebration Dinner, where Father Christmas voted Holly and me Christmas Elves of the Year for saving Christmas. As I said in my speech, it was like a dream come true.

Afterwards, Father Christmas tapped me on the shoulder and whispered, 'I've got someone who'd like to meet you, if you don't mind?'

I looked down to see his grandson Sprig, dressed in his finest red velvet and holding the lemur I had made for him.

'Can I have your autograph?' he squeaked.

'Of course,' I said with a wink.

'Thanks,' whispered Father Christmas. 'You've made one grandfather extremely popular. And by the way, handmade toys are going to be a bigger part of operations next year. Machines have their place, but you know the most important ingredient in a toy?'

'Stuffing!' piped Sprig.

'I was thinking of love,' chuckled Father Christmas. 'But have it your way.'

But as happy as all that made me, it was nothing next to the news that Holly wanted to partner me in the Boxing Day Pairs Competition!

Tomorrow morning we're going out to the glacier first thing, so we can practise without anyone watching.

I'm going to have to learn Max's part, which is really tricky, so wish us luck!

I'll let you know how it went.

CONTINUE THE
CHRISTMAS MAGIC
WITH AN EXTRACT FROM

'A sheer delight for kids both big and Small'
Ruth Jones, Award-winning writer and comedian

The
Night I Met
Father
Christmas

The bestselling author actor and comedian
BEN MILLER

Chapter One

When I was small, one of my friends said something really silly. He said that Father Christmas didn't exist.

'So where do all the Christmas presents come from?' I asked him. He didn't have an answer.

'I don't know,' he said. 'It's just something my older sister told me.'

'Who comes down the chimney and eats the mince pies and drinks the brandy?' I asked. 'Who rides the sleigh?'

My friend was silent for a while.

'You know what?' he said. 'You're right. I don't know why I brought it up. Do you want to play marbles?'

That night, I had trouble getting to sleep. I had won the argument, but my friend had planted a tiny seed of doubt in my mind. What if Father Christmas *wasn't* real?

As Christmas approached, I began to ask myself all sorts of worrying questions: who *was* Father Christmas? Why did he bring presents? How did he deliver them all in one night? How did it all start?

I made up my mind that there was only one way to find out the truth. I had to meet Father Christmas, face to face.

Of course, I didn't tell anyone about my plan. My parents would have tried to stop me, and my twin sisters would have wanted to tag along, even though they were much too young. This was a serious operation and I couldn't risk it going wrong.

Finally, Christmas Eve arrived, and my parents came up to kiss me goodnight.

'Do you know what day it is tomorrow?' asked my mother, her eyes twinkling.

'Is it Wednesday?' I asked, pretending not to care.

She looked at my father, who shrugged.

'Yes, darling,' she said, trying to maintain an air of suspense. 'It is Wednesday. But it's also Christmas Day.'

'Oh,' I said. 'I'm not really that interested in Christmas.'

'Really?' said my father. They both looked very disappointed, and for a very brief moment I felt bad for tricking them.

'It's okay, I suppose,' I said, 'if you like presents and chocolate and sweets and things like that, but I prefer to work through a few maths problems while listening to classical music.' And then I faked a big yawn and closed my eyes.

'Whatever makes you happy, darling,' said my mother, sounding worried. They kissed me goodnight, switched out the light, and went downstairs.

I lay there in the dark, with my eyes closed, listening. I could hear my sisters in their bedroom down the hall, talking in their own special made-up language, which only they could understand. Usually, when I heard them talking like that it made me feel a bit left out, but not tonight, because I knew that I was doing something very special.

Eventually, my sisters fell quiet and the house suddenly seemed very deep and dark. I could hear the low murmur of my parents talking downstairs, but soon that stopped too, and then the stairs creaked as they made their way up to bed.

I knew they might look in on me, so I acted as if I was fast asleep.

'Goodnight, little man,' my father whispered, as he gently moved my head back on to the pillow and pulled the covers up to keep me warm. Then I smelled my mother's perfume as she gave me a kiss. The door closed, and I heard their footsteps crossing the landing to their bedroom.

I lay still, listening in the darkness. After what felt like the longest time, I decided it was safe enough to half-open one eye. My bedside clock showed a quarter to twelve. I had never, ever been awake that late before, and I wondered for a moment if, when it struck midnight, I would be turned to stone, like a child in a fairy tale.

I pulled back the covers, swung my feet

down on to the rug and tiptoed to the window. Outside, the window ledge was covered in snow. The moon was thin but bright, and in our neighbour's garden a fox picked its way across the white lawn. Above me, the blue-black sky was scattered with stars and little wisps of cloud. Nothing moved. No shooting stars, no satellites, not even a trundling planet. And definitely no reindeer-drawn sleigh.

I slunk back into bed. Using both pillows, together with one of the cushions from the chair, I made a sort of bed-throne, so that I could sit up and watch the open sky. Whatever happened, I wasn't going to sleep. I was going to wait until Father Christmas came.

Author photo © Faye Thomas

BEN MILLER is the bestselling author
of magical stories for all the family:
The Night I Met Father Christmas,
The Boy Who Made the World Disappear, The Day I Fell
Into a Fairytale, How I Became a Dog Called Midnight
and *Diary of a Christmas Elf.*

He is an actor, director and comedian, best-known for the
Armstrong and Miller sketch show, the Johnny English and
Paddington films, BBC's Death in Paradise and
recent Netflix smash, Bridgerton.

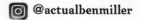 @actualbenmiller

ENTER A
WORLD OF WONDER
WITH CLASSIC ADVENTURE FROM BESTSELLING
BEN MILLER

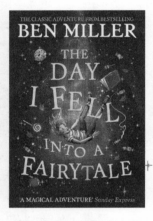

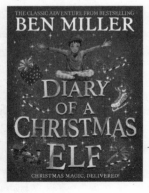